THE SMURFS ™

publications international, ltd.

D0603743

All of the Smurfs of Smurf Village work hard to prepare for the Blue Moon Festival. Even Grouchy Smurf admits that this is a very special time. Look around to find Grouchy and some of his friends.

Papa Smurf

Grouchy Smurf

Brainy Smurf

Smurfette

Gutsy Smurf

Clumsy Smurf

Clumsy Smurf defeated Gargamel! Still, some of the Smurfs are nervous to dance next to him. Look around the Blue Moon Festival to find these Smurfs that he has already bumped into.

Smurf back to Smurf Village and search out these smurfberry treats.

Smurfberry ice cream

Smurfberry shortcake

Smurfberry cobbler

Smurfberry pudding

Smurfberry pie

Smurfberry cookies

Smurfberry tart

Stroll back to Central Park to find these things that Gargamel might want to add to his wardrobe.

This medallion

These gloves

This robe

This hat

This magic wand

These boots

The Smurfs like to eat all kinds of different foods, but they need smurfberries to keep their strength up. Cruise back to the kitchen and find two dozen smurfberries.

Each Smurf has just one outfit to wear, so Smurfette can't believe her eyes when she sees rows and rows of dresses that are just her size. Smurf back to the toy store to find these dresses that catch her eye.

Go back to the busy city street to find six Anjelou ads featuring a blue moon.

When Gargamel gets to Dr. Wong's, he will pick out a new wand for himself. Scoot back to the shop to find the wand and these other items on display.

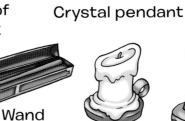

Bottle of red ink

Crystal pendant

Wand

Candle

Statue of a wizard

Eye of newt

Quill

Head back to the battle scene to spot these things from the Winslows' apartment that the Smurfs used against Gargamel.

ngernail file

Apple with needles

Letter opener

Sharpened pencil

Big pin

Lobster fork

Jokey Smurf thinks that a party is a perfect occasion for playing pranks! Boogie back to the Blue Moon Festival to find eight of his exploding gifts.

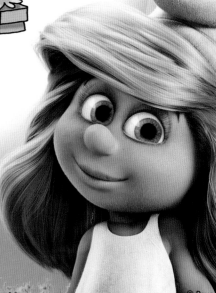